OVERCOMING ADVERSITY:
SHARING THE AMERICAN DREAM

NORAH JONES

MASON CREST PUBLISHERS
PHILADELPHIA

OVERCOMING ADVERSITY: SHARING THE AMERICAN DREAM

Charles Barkley
Halle Berry
Cesar Chavez
Kenny Chesney
George Clooney
Johnny Depp
Tony Dungy
Jermaine Dupri
Jennifer Garner
Kevin Garnett
John B. Herrington
Salma Hayek
Vanessa Hudgens
Samuel L. Jackson

Norah Jones
Martin Lawrence
Bruce Lee
Eva Longoria
Malcolm X
Carlos Mencia
Chuck Norris
Barack Obama
Rosa Parks
Bill Richardson
Russell Simmons
Carrie Underwood
Modern American Indian Leaders

**OVERCOMING ADVERSITY:
SHARING THE AMERICAN DREAM**

NORAH JONES

DONNA LATHAM

**MASON CREST PUBLISHERS
PHILADELPHIA**

ABOUT CROSS-CURRENTS

When you see this logo, turn to the Cross-Currents section at the back of the book. The Cross-Currents features explore connections between people, places, events, and ideas.

Produced by OTTN Publishing, Stockton, New Jersey

Mason Crest Publishers
370 Reed Road
Broomall, PA 19008
www.masoncrest.com

Copyright © 2009 by Mason Crest Publishers. All rights reserved.
Printed and bound in the United States.

First printing

1 3 5 7 9 8 6 4 2

Library of Congress Cataloging-in-Publication Data

Latham, Donna.
  Norah Jones / Donna Latham.
     p. cm. — (Sharing the American dream : overcoming adversity)
  Includes bibliographical references, discography, filmography, and index.
  ISBN 978-1-4222-0590-7 (hc) — ISBN 978-1-4222-0751-2 (pb)
 1. Jones, Norah, 1979–Juvenile literature. 2. Singers—United
States—Biography—Juvenile literature. I. Title.
  ML3930.J626L37 2008
  782.42164092—dc22
     [B]
                              2008022991

TABLE OF CONTENTS

Chapter One: Grammy Awards Sweep	**6**
Chapter Two: Blooming in Grapevine	**12**
Chapter Three: From Coffeehouse Singer to International Superstar	**18**
Chapter Four: New Music	**26**
Chapter Five: Branching Out and Moving On	**34**
Cross-Currents	**42**
Chronology	**50**
Accomplishments/Awards	**52**
Further Reading	**54**
Internet Resources	**55**
Glossary	**56**
Chapter Notes	**58**
Index	**61**

CHAPTER ONE

GRAMMY AWARDS SWEEP

Outside Madison Square Garden, winter gripped New York City. Inside the famous arena, the atmosphere was sizzling. It was February 23, 2003, and some of the biggest names in the music industry had gathered for the 45th Grammy Awards. Live performances were interspersed with the presentation of the prestigious awards.

The evening opened on a nostalgic note, as Paul Simon and Art Garfunkel—a popular pair who had broken up in 1970—reunited to perform their 1966 hit "The Sound of Silence." Simon & Garfunkel received a special award for lifetime achievement at the 45th Grammy Awards. A bit later, the up-and-coming British band Coldplay took the stage. Accompanied by the New York Philharmonic, Coldplay moved the crowd at Madison Square Garden—and millions of TV viewers around the world—with a stirring rendition of their song "Politik." Even in the huge arena, 25-year-old John Mayer managed to create a sense of intimacy

READ MORE

To learn about the Grammy Awards, which recognize outstanding achievements in the recording industry, turn to page 42.

Grammy Awards Sweep

Norah Jones performs her single "Don't Know Why" during the 45th Grammy Awards, February 23, 2003. Though her debut album was released on a small label, her sound was mellow, and she didn't sell records with sexy videos or outrageous behavior, Norah took the music industry by storm.

with his acoustic hit "Your Body Is a Wonderland." Another highlight was a tribute to Joe Strummer, who had died just two months earlier. Veteran rockers Bruce Springsteen, Elvis Costello, Dave Grohl, Tony Kanal, and Steven Van Zandt teamed up for a rollicking version of "London Calling," a song Strummer had cowritten and performed with his legendary punk band the Clash.

"This Is Freakin' Me Out"

When it came time to present Record of the Year honors—the first major prize of the 45th Grammy Awards—Aretha Franklin and Bonnie Raitt strode to center stage. The two renowned singers took turns announcing the nominees. Vanessa Carlton smiled slightly when Raitt announced her song "A Thousand Miles." A jittery Eminem, nominated for "Without Me," licked his lips and shifted restlessly as Franklin called out his name. Norah Jones, a doe-eyed newcomer nominated for her hit "Don't Know Why," raised her eyebrows and shrugged when the TV cameras focused on her. Nelly sat expressionless behind dark shades as his "Dilemma" was announced. The guys in Nickelback grinned in obvious enjoyment when Franklin named "How You Remind Me."

The five nominees introduced, Franklin proceeded to announce the winner. "And the Grammy goes to . . . Norah Jones!"

The petite, raven-haired singer rose from her seat. She motioned for the producers of "Don't Know Why," Arif Mardin and Jay Newland, to join her in accepting the award. Onstage, Raitt and Franklin each gave Norah a brief hug. Like a star-stuck

> **READ MORE**
> Legions of music fans know her as "the Queen of Soul." To learn more about recording legend Aretha Franklin, turn to page 43.

fan, Norah shook her head in disbelief. The 23-year-old seemed stunned to be in the presence of these music legends, both of whom had been inducted into the Rock and Roll Hall of Fame.

"I can't believe this," Norah said, one hand fluttering while the other grasped her Grammy statuette. "Bonnie Raitt and Aretha Franklin? This is freakin' me out." The crowd at Madison Square Garden laughed at Norah's wide-eyed wonderment.

Many people in the audience, as well as many watching the Grammy Awards on TV, were getting their first glimpse of the young singer. But Norah Jones's smooth and sultry voice was already familiar to a host of music fans. Norah's debut album, *Come Away with Me*, had been released on a small record label and with little fanfare in late February 2002. Music critics raved about the newcomer's confident, mature style. The single "Don't

Norah Jones accepts the Record of the Year Grammy, for "Don't Know Why." Producer Arif Mardin stands between presenters Aretha Franklin (in white dress) and Bonnie Raitt.

Know Why" began receiving some airplay on jazz and adult-contemporary radio stations, and even without a slick publicity campaign or big arena concerts, sales of *Come Away with Me* began to take off. Within three months of its release, the album had gone gold—that is, it had sold 500,000 copies in the United States. By August 2002 it had hit the platinum mark (1 million copies). In late January 2003, Norah's album reached #1 on the *Billboard* 200 charts. By the time of the Grammy Awards ceremony, more than 4 million people had bought *Come Away with Me*.

"All the Cake"

The Grammy Awards would introduce even more fans to the music of Norah Jones. Norah had received five Grammy nominations. In addition to Record of the Year, she was nominated for Album of the Year, Best New Artist, Best Pop Vocal Album, and Best Female Pop Vocal Performance. Norah recorded a clean sweep, taking home all five of the Grammys for which she was nominated. In addition, *Come Away with Me* was nominated for and won three other Grammys. Jesse Harris, who wrote "Don't Know Why," garnered Song of the Year honors. Producer Arif Mardin collected the Grammy in the Best Produced Album, Non-Classical category. And engineers S. Husky Hoskulds and Jay Newland won for Best Engineered Album, Non-Classical.

In the midst of her incredibly successful evening, Norah Jones remained modest and gracious. "I feel really blessed and really lucky," she said after beating out a strong field that included Bruce Springsteen's *The Rising* and Eminem's *The Eminem Show* to win the Grammy for Album of the Year.

Such humility is typical of Norah Jones. Of her Grammy sweep, Norah would later say, a bit sheepishly, "I felt like I went to somebody else's birthday party and I ate all their cake. Without anybody else getting a piece."

Grammy Awards Sweep 11

Norah poses with her five Grammy statuettes. The humble singer and pianist likened her 2003 Grammy sweep to going to someone else's birthday party and eating all the cake.

CHAPTER TWO

BLOOMING IN GRAPEVINE

Geetanjali Norah Jones Shankar—who would shorten her name to Norah Jones at age 16—was born in Brooklyn, New York, on March 30, 1979. Her parents, Sue Jones and Ravi Shankar, were both deeply involved in music. Jones was a concert promoter. Shankar was a renowned sitar player from India. He had gained international fame when he taught the traditional Indian instrument to, and became a close friend of, George Harrison of the Beatles.

Though Sue Jones and Ravi Shankar had a nine-year relationship, they never married. And shortly after the birth of their daughter, the couple split up. At the time, Shankar was involved with at least two other women.

Norah knew her father and visited him from time to time when she was young. But Sue Jones grew increasingly resentful of Shankar, and when Norah was nine, Jones left New York and went to Texas with her daughter. She didn't tell Shankar about the cross-country move, and Norah would have no further contact with her father until she turned 18.

> **READ MORE**
> Turn to page 44 for a brief profile of Norah Jones's father, Ravi Shankar.

The Joneses settled into a modest home in Grapevine, a suburb of Dallas. There Sue worked as a nurse and struggled to raise her daughter as a single mom. The two had a very close relationship—

Norah Jones's father, the Indian sitar virtuoso Ravi Shankar, stands behind his friend and pupil George Harrison in this 1975 photo. Shankar and Norah's mother, Sue Jones, never married, and Norah would long resent her famous father.

and today Norah remains close to her mother, whom she speaks with almost daily and has called her "guiding light."

Musical Gifts

Norah had shown musical promise from an early age. At five, she'd begun singing in church choirs. By seven, she was taking piano lessons, and she later played the alto sax.

As she grew up in Texas, Norah absorbed a wide variety of musical influences. At the age of 13, as she was looking through her mother's large and diverse collection of records, Norah stumbled upon an album by the legendary jazz singer Billie Holiday. Believing Billie to be a man's name, Norah was surprised to hear a woman's voice when she played the record. Holiday's unique vocal stylings enthralled the young teen. Norah would later confess that she consciously tried to imitate Holiday. In addition to Billie Holiday, Norah's favorite performers included Ray Charles and Stevie Wonder, two accomplished piano players whose music embraced soul, R&B, jazz, and funk; country stars Johnny Cash, Willie Nelson, and Dolly Parton; and singer/songwriter Joni Mitchell, a folk music icon. All influenced Norah's musical path.

During the summers of 1994 and 1995, Norah attended Interlochen Arts Camp in northwestern Michigan. The prestigious summer camp has been training young musicians and artists since the 1920s. While at Interlochen, Norah took jazz classes. She also met and became friends with a young flute player named Daru Oda. Years later, the two would form a band together.

READ MORE
For a short biography of jazz legend Billie Holiday, see page 45.

"One of the Coolest Things"

When Norah was 15, she and her mother moved to central

Dallas. Norah transferred from Grapevine High School, where she had completed ninth grade, to Booker T. Washington High School for the Performing and Visual Arts. A magnet school for youth who aspire to careers in music, dance, theater, or painting, Booker T. Washington is small and accepts only the most gifted students.

Norah loved the atmosphere at her high school. "It's probably one of the coolest things I've ever gotten to do," she said of her years at Booker T. Washington. "I was surrounded by people my own age who were doing all these crazy, creative things. There were dancers dancing down the hallway and singers singing everywhere."

Norah had won acceptance into Booker T. Washington on the strength of her piano skills. But she also blossomed as a singer. During her high school career, Norah received three *DownBeat* Student Music Awards—for Best Original Composition (1996) and Best Jazz Vocalist (1996 and 1997). *DownBeat*, considered the premier jazz magazine in the country, has sponsored the Student Music Awards since the late 1970s. All recordings entered in the annual competition are judged by the magazine's editors and professional musicians,

Norah (center) played saxophone in the eighth-grade concert band at Colleyville Middle School. Later, at the prestigious Booker T. Washington High School for the Performing and Visual Arts in Dallas, Norah would concentrate on the piano.

so being selected for an award is quite an honor for a student musician.

During her high school years, Norah performed her first professional gigs. She sang at coffeehouses, pocketing a hundred dollars a pop.

Family Ties

In 1997, when Norah was 18, she decided to contact her father. At the time, Ravi Shankar was living in California with his second wife and their daughter, Anoushka. Norah tracked down the phone number. Anoushka, who was then 16, answered the phone when Norah called. "A soft-spoken girl on the other end

Norah Jones (left) with Anoushka Shankar, 2003. The sisters had no contact until Norah was 18 years old, but they quickly developed a close bond.

of the phone asked to speak to Mr. Ravi Shankar," Anoushka recalled. "When she said who she was I was stunned because by then I had totally given up on the idea that we would ever have any contact with her."

The half sisters soon met. They hit if off immediately and have since remained close. It took much longer for Norah to reconcile with her father, whom she greatly resented for the way he had treated her mother.

> **READ MORE**
> Nora Jones's half sister, Anoushka, is a successful musician in her own right. For details, see page 46.

"A Jazz Snob"

After graduating from high school, Norah enrolled at the University of North Texas (UNT), which is located about 35 miles north of Dallas, in Denton. Although various musical styles would find their way into Norah's later records, in college she immersed herself completely in jazz. "I used to be a jazz snob, believe it or not," she confessed. "I sort of turned my nose up at anything more commercial." At UNT, she majored in jazz piano, performed with a jazz piano ensemble, and sang with the university's jazz singers.

Norah paid the rent with gigs at weddings, private parties, and restaurants. She enjoyed a two-year run playing the piano at Popolo's, an Italian restaurant in Dallas. "Usually people didn't listen to the music because they were too busy eating their dinner," Norah recalled. "But some nights they would listen. And I'd think, 'What can I play next to keep them clapping?'" After moving back to her hometown, Norah would find out.

CHAPTER THREE

FROM COFFEEHOUSE SINGER TO INTERNATIONAL SUPERSTAR

During the summer of 1999, after her sophomore year at the University of North Texas, Norah Jones went to New York City. She intended to return to Texas in the fall. But Norah immediately fell in love with the city and its quirky music scene. As summer came to a close, the 20-year-old decided to drop out of school and remain in New York to pursue a professional music career.

Norah settled in Greenwich Village, an artsy area in Manhattan's Lower West Side. Although she lived in a small loft apartment, money was tight. During the day, Norah worked as a waitress in the Metropolitan Art Gallery's café, earning $2.00 an hour plus tips. At night, she picked up gigs playing piano or singing in coffeehouses, restaurants, and lounges.

Music wasn't the main attraction of these tiny venues. Rather, the music was intended as a pleasant background for patrons as they chatted with friends and drank lattes, sipped wine, or ate dinner. Norah's laid-back style might have been well suited for this sort of environment, but she sometimes grew frustrated that people weren't listening to her.

Gigs at small music clubs afforded Norah the opportunity to be a bit louder and showier. For several years, she performed with a variety of local bands. She experimented with flashy vocals but ultimately didn't like the results. "I sang in some bad blues bands for a while," Norah told Jon Pareles of the *New York Times,* "and

Norah Jones on a rooftop in New York City, 2003. Four years earlier, after her sophomore year in college, Norah had moved to New York to pursue a music career.

I heard a recording of myself. I thought, 'God, I'm over singing, and I don't sound like Aretha Franklin, so I shouldn't try.'"

The Handsome Band Forms

The group of musicians who would back Norah Jones on her first albums, called the Handsome Band, came together by chance. In 1999, shortly after arriving in New York, Norah had met Adam Levy. Levy was an experienced jazz guitarist who had recently moved to New York from San Francisco. Friends introduced him to Norah. Though he'd never heard her sing or play piano, Levy gave Norah his phone number and told her to call him if she ever needed a guitar player.

Several months later, Norah did give Levy a call. She had a gig to play at a little art gallery inside a Mercedes car dealership. They didn't have a chance to rehearse beforehand, but when Levy finally did hear Norah sing at the gallery, he was astonished. "People are dipping celery sticks into spinach dip and sipping champagne out of plastic cups, generally ignoring us," the guitarist would recall, "and I'm standing there playing guitar behind Norah and going, 'Whoa. Something really different is going on here.' . . . That gig was some of the best ignored music I've ever made."

Later, when Norah asked Levy about bass players, he gave her a list of bassists he knew. Levy's list was alphabetical, so the first person Norah called was Lee Alexander. He agreed to play a gig but didn't expect much musically from Norah. "She was playing a Sunday brunch at the Washington Square Hotel," Alexander recalled. "I wasn't really excited, and I had another gig that morning. . . . I was, like, forty minutes late. They were already playing. I started unpacking my bass, and then I thought, 'Wow. She can actually sing.'" Alexander joined Norah's band, and he would also become her long-term boyfriend.

Norah picked up another member of the Handsome Band through a chance encounter on a Greenwich Village street. One day, as Norah lugged an amp down the street, another young woman was approaching from the opposite direction. The woman had a vaguely familiar face. Norah gawked. The woman stared back. As they passed, the two remembered each other at the same time. They had been friends years earlier at summer band camp at Interlochen. Norah and Daru Oda—who had just moved to New York from Chicago—hung out with each other and got caught up. Oda became a backup singer in Norah's band.

Big Break

Around the same time Norah Jones was reconnecting with Daru Oda, another friend landed a songwriting contract with Sony Music. Norah and Jesse Harris had first met while she was a student at the University of North Texas and he was a guitarist for a jazz band that visited the UNT campus. Now the native New Yorker was looking for a female vocalist to sing his mellow new tune "Don't Know Why." He asked Norah Jones, and she agreed.

Norah Jones and Lee Alexander lived in the two-bedroom apartment above this Brooklyn barbershop until February 2003. The day after the Grammy Awards, however, a New York newspaper printed Norah's address, and a large crowd of celebrity watchers assembled on the sidewalk. Norah and her boyfriend soon moved to Manhattan to regain their privacy.

Harris booked some gigs at the Living Room, an intimate little club. With Lee Alexander backing her on bass and Jesse Harris taking on guitar duties, Norah had a blast. And her subtle presence mesmerized audiences at the Living Room. People were finally listening to her music rather than regarding it simply as pleasant background noise.

In a roundabout way, Norah soon came to the attention of Blue Note Records, a small jazz label established in 1939. A friend of Lee Alexander's brought his wife, who worked at Blue Note's parent company, to the Living Room one night. Impressed by Norah's performance, she arranged for the young vocalist to meet the president of Blue Note, Bruce Lundvall.

Before they are signed to recording contracts, aspiring singers and bands typically make demo CDs to showcase their music. Often these CDs are produced in a studio and have a well-engineered sound—the better to grab the interest of record company executives and talent scouts. When Norah Jones sat down with Bruce Lundvall on March 31, 2000—just a day after her 21st birthday—she had no such demo to share with the Blue Note president. She admitted that she hadn't really been thinking about a recording contract yet—in fact, she wasn't even sure what sort of music she would like to do. All Norah had for Lundvall to hear were three raw recordings of her singing. Still, he was intrigued. Over the following months, Blue Note representatives checked out several of Norah's live shows. Liking what they saw and heard, they decided to pay for Norah to record some demo tracks.

In August 2000, Norah and her band headed into the studio. The first song they tackled was "Don't Know Why." It came together perfectly. "First take, all live, completely like random," Norah recalled. "We didn't know what the drummer was going to play till we played it." After Norah had laid down about a dozen demo tracks, Bruce Lundvall decided she was the real deal and signed her to a record contract.

Norah kept her day job as a waitress while she recorded her debut album. Her expectations for *Come Away with Me*, released in February 2002, were modest: she hoped it would sell 10,000 copies. Instead—paced by the single "Don't Know Why" and boosted by Norah's 2003 Grammy sweep—*Come Away with Me* would eventually sell more than 2,000 times that number. Worldwide sales exceeded 20 million copies, with over 10 million of that total coming in U.S. sales.

"Beyond Category"

Critics and ordinary fans alike praised Norah's music, but they had a hard time categorizing it. Although Blue Note is a jazz label, *Come Away with Me* wasn't really a jazz album. It was more of a jazz-influenced pop album, with bits of soul, blues, folk, and country mixed in. Some said the album was "bluesy jazz"; others, "folksy jazz." One writer suggested that, in the manner of the great Duke Ellington, "Norah Jones is truly beyond category and she is without genre."

The 14 songs on *Come Away with Me* were mostly well-crafted and mellow romantic ballads. The arrangements were clean and spare. What most distinguished the album—and what captivated listeners—was Norah's singing. Her delivery was relaxed and natural. She steered clear of the pitch-shifting vocal theatrics that were much in vogue with other female singers. Some critics heard echoes of the great Billie Holiday in Norah's slightly husky voice and her mature, confident style—which was especially noteworthy because Norah was just 22 years old when she recorded the album.

The Downside of Fame

As *Come Away with Me* began to take off, Norah and the Handsome Band hit the road, playing to packed houses in cities across the United States. Tours of Europe, Asia, and Australia followed. Everywhere the band went, reporters clamored to

Norah Jones in concert with the Handsome Band in Pula, Croatia. After the 2003 release of *Come Away with Me*, Norah and her band mates kept up a grueling performance schedule that took them on tours through the United States, Europe, Asia, and Australia.

interview Norah. Most asked about her famous father, a subject Norah preferred to avoid.

Eventually, the pressures of the grueling performance schedule and the constant glare of the media spotlight began to take a toll on the young singer, who is somewhat reserved by nature. She felt oppressed by all the hype. She bristled at the endless questions about Ravi Shankar. She worried about becoming overexposed—a concern that seemed quite justified after a dance remix was made of "Don't Know Why." An exasperated Norah vetoed the song's release.

"I was so overwhelmed that I became almost anesthetized to it," Norah said of her sudden fame. "I mean . . . it all seemed so ridiculous. It was a total circus; it was too much. At a certain point it starts to take you away from the music. And the music is the whole point."

CHAPTER FOUR

NEW MUSIC

During the spring of 2003, Norah returned to New York after an exhausting year on the road. But she wasn't planning to simply kick back and relax. She and the Handsome Band headed into the studio to record a second album, which Blue Note Records planned to release at Christmas.

Norah wasn't totally happy with the results of the recording session. Because she and her band mates were already committed to another packed schedule of live shows over the summer, the release date of Norah's second album had to be pushed back. Norah found time to polish the arrangements to her satisfaction in the fall, and a February 2004 release was announced.

Another Big Success

In its first week, *Feels Like Home* sold more than a million copies in the United States, rocketing to #1 on the *Billboard* 200 chart. U.S. sales would ultimately top 4 million, with approximately 2 million additional copies sold overseas.

Feels Like Home had the same mellow, easygoing feel that had helped make *Come Away with Me* such a runaway success. Yet it was a bit more upbeat, a bit more country, and considerably

New Music

Norah and one of her musical inspirations, Dolly Parton, perform at Nashville's Grand Ole Opry, November 5, 2003. Norah's second album, *Feels Like Home*, included a duet with Parton—the lively country tune "Creepin' In."

quirkier. On "Creepin' In," a bouncy bluegrass ditty, Norah sang a duet with one of her early musical inspirations, Dolly Parton. The two women recorded the song live in a single take. On "Don't Miss You at All," Norah added her own lyrics to a Duke Ellington melody. She also covered a song by the gravel-voiced Tom Waits, and another by folk/country balladeer Townes Van Zandt.

But most of the songs on *Feels Like Home* were written or

READ MORE

Dolly Parton landed her first recording contract in 1959, at the age of 13. To learn more about this country music legend, turn to page 48.

cowritten by Norah and members of the Handsome Band. In fact, all of Norah's band mates—bassist Lee Alexander, guitar player Adam Levy, drummer Andy Borger, and backup vocalist Daru Oda—had at least one song on the album. This, Norah told an interviewer, made *Feels Like Home* "kind of special for us. . . . It's a very family kind of band. I mean we're all very close."

Snorah Jones?

Norah may have been happy with the way her second album turned out—and fans certainly responded favorably, giving Blue Note Records another big moneymaker. But not all music critics were fond of *Feels Like Home*. Some complained that it was too similar to *Come Away with Me*. Others likened Norah's sound to bland, sleep-inducing "elevator music"—and referred to her jokingly as "Snorah Jones."

Ben Ratliff of the *New York Times* grumbled that Norah's songs lacked emotional depth. "Nothing much happens in a Norah Jones song," Ratliff asserted, "whether she writes it or not. . . . She reflects, she wonders, she grows wistful; she considers falling in or out of love, and when she pledges it . . . she does so in certifiable clichés about skies falling and butterflies." While he acknowledged Norah's vocal abilities, Ratliff believed she was "hiding out" in innocuous, low-key music. He wished she would abandon this commercially successful formula and take some chances musically.

Norah had little time to worry about such criticisms. She and the Handsome Band were on tour throughout 2004. And between the concert performances, Norah had to sit down for a host of interviews and make countless media appearances.

Finally, in the spring of 2005, Norah decided that it was time to slow down. The previous three years had been a nearly continuous blur of touring and promotional events. Norah would admit that, while she was grateful for her success, she didn't enjoy all the stress.

Time to Relax

Back at home in New York City, Norah shed the life of a superstar musician and settled into the role of regular person. She cooked. She watched movies. She enjoyed life off the road with her boyfriend, Lee Alexander. Norah hung out with her friends, shooting pool and going to small clubs. Despite her fame, she could still walk around New York City without attracting much attention. "I'm kind of nerdy and unfashionable," she told an interviewer, "so people don't give a second look."

Though Norah was temporarily through with the commitments of the music industry, her love of music had by no means dimmed. She enjoyed watching fellow musicians perform in New York City clubs. And, concealing her identity with makeup and outrageous costumes (including a blonde wig), Norah played guitar and sang in a garage band that also included Daru Oda and Andy Borger. Norah also joined Lee Alexander and three other musicians in a country band called the Little Willies (whose name was a tribute to Willie Nelson). The Little Willies released a self-titled album in 2006.

A Different Side

Refreshed and revitalized by her time off, Norah set to work on a new album. Unlike her first two releases, this album would be made up entirely of songs she wrote or cowrote (often with Lee Alexander). Arif Mardin—who had produced *Come Away with Me* and *Feels Like Home*—died in 2006, so Alexander took over the duties of producer. Alexander brought the musicians into the home studio he shared with Norah. Much of the album was

The Little Willies began as a tribute band to country legend Willie Nelson. The band members are, from left: Dan Rieser, Lee Alexander, Richard Julian, Norah Jones, and Jim Campilongo.

recorded there, giving it an intimate feel. *Not Too Late* was released by Blue Note Records on January 30, 2007.

This time, critics didn't complain that Norah's music was bland, emotionally shallow, or safe. Norah had abandoned her standard fare of romantic ballads to explore serious themes such as politics, war, and death. *Not Too Late* also had some wry humor and a bit of mildly suggestive material.

Reviewers heralded a more mature Norah Jones. Jon Pareles of the *New York Times* was typical. He called *Not Too Late* "darker, thornier, and sometimes funnier than the albums that made her a star."

Norah was quick to point out that her earlier albums—many of whose songs were written by others—didn't necessarily represent her personality or outlook. "You listen to my first album and you get a perception of me: very romantic, melancholy, sort of wispy," she noted. "It bothered me for a long time, because that's never been my personality." If her early music was always mellow and sweet, Norah admitted that she was fun loving and could be loud and obnoxious.

Yet Norah also insisted that the darker songs she had written for *Not Too Late* weren't evidence of a dark, brooding personality.

Released in January 2007, *Not Too Late* represented a musical departure for Norah Jones. Whereas her first two albums had been filled with romantic ballads, *Not Too Late* explored themes such as politics, war, and death. Norah wrote or cowrote all 13 songs on the album.

Rather, Norah said, she simply wanted to express in song some of the disturbing things she saw around her.

The war in Iraq and the presidency of George W. Bush inspired several of the songs on *Not Too Late*. On the album's first track, "Wish I Could," a woman mourns a boyfriend lost to war. Norah said she wrote the song while thinking about a soldier she had once dated. She tried unsuccessfully to find him and feared that he might have been killed overseas.

The second song on the album was a slow and sparse number called "Sinkin' Soon." It seemed to evoke President Bush's woeful leadership, as Norah crooned:

> In a boat that's built of sticks and hay,
> We drifted from the shore,
> With a captain who's too proud to say,
> That he dropped the oar,
> Now a tiny hole has sprung a leak,
> In this cheap pontoon,
> Now the hull has started growing weak,
> And we're gonna be sinkin' soon.

"My Dear Country," written in 2004, expressed Norah's dismay with the reelection of President Bush. "[N]othing is as scary as election day," Norah sang.

> But the day after is darker,
> And darker and darker it goes,
> Who knows, maybe the plan will change,
> Who knows, maybe he's not deranged.

In February 2007, a few weeks after the release of *Not Too Late*, the CBS news program *60 Minutes* aired an interview with

Norah Jones by correspondent Katie Couric. Norah admitted that she really didn't know where her career was headed, but she wasn't worried about her album sales. "I don't expect to sell millions of records every time. I just don't think that's gonna be possible."

Although it certainly didn't approach the commercial success of *Come Away with Me*—and fell short of *Feels Like Home*—*Not Too Late* did in fact sell millions of records. Within two months of its release, the album had been certified double platinum.

CHAPTER FIVE

BRANCHING OUT AND MOVING ON

In 2006 Wong Kar-wai, a filmmaker from Hong Kong, called Norah Jones and said he wanted to talk with her. Norah wasn't familiar with Wong or his work, but she agreed to meet him at a coffeehouse.

After some small talk, the director asked Norah whether she wanted to act. "I thought, 'If I say no, I might regret it,'" Norah recalled. "And if I say yes, I'll have an experience. If I stink, whatever! I'm a musician—I've got a day job. What can I lose here?"

A New Role

Wong tapped Norah for a starring role in his movie *My Blueberry Nights*. She would play a waitress in New York City who, after a breakup with her boyfriend, travels somewhat aimlessly across the country. Finally, she returns to New York and finds love with the owner of a café she used to frequent.

Although Norah had never acted before, Wong instructed her not to take acting lessons. He wanted her to be natural.

Norah admitted that she was nervous and doubtful of her abilities during the early stages of filming, but this actually helped her. At the start of the story, her character lacks confidence and is a bit lost. Norah was able to tap into her own anxiety to convey her

This movie poster for *My Blueberry Nights* featured the three female leads (clockwise from top right): Rachel Weisz, Natalie Portman, and Norah Jones. Norah played a waitress who wanders across the country after breaking up with her boyfriend.

character's angst. As the filming progressed, Norah gained more confidence as an actress, which mirrored her character's growing self-assurance.

My Blueberry Nights featured a talented cast, including Natalie Portman, Rachel Weisz, David Strathairn, and Jude Law. These veteran actors did their best to put Norah at ease, telling her they were fans of her music. "It's like playing with a great band—they just make you look better," Norah said of her costars.

My Blueberry Nights premiered at the Cannes Film Festival in May 2007. The highly anticipated film didn't play well with the

Norah and *My Blueberry Nights* costar Jude Law on opening night at the 60th Cannes Film Festival, May 16, 2007. The critical response to Norah's motion picture debut was mostly lukewarm.

critics, however. Many found the story syrupy sweet and with little substance.

Nor were the critics overwhelmed by Norah's performance. "Ms. Jones, whose diffidence lends her musical performances an air of intrigue and seduction, does not so much fail to act as refuse to try," wrote A. O. Scott in the *New York Times*. "Her face registers degrees of strickenness and bewilderment, but she is most persuasive when she falls asleep at the counter of [a diner] after gorging on pie."

Michael Phillips of the *Chicago Tribune* had a similar evaluation. Norah Jones "may be a ripe camera subject," Phillips wrote, "but isn't yet an actress."

Surviving a Breakup

The year 2007, in addition to bringing Norah's first foray into film, also brought the end of a long relationship. She and Lee Alexander called it quits. Their breakup was friendly, and they planned to continue their working relationship. "We will always be good friends," Norah told an interviewer, "but we have worked together, lived together, and been on the road together. We have known each other for seven and a half years, which is a quarter of my life. I think we both agree it has run its course."

Now on her own, Norah kept busy with her various musical ventures. She continued to moonlight with the Little Willies, her country band. Willie Nelson himself joined the band onstage a few times. The Little Willies had started as a cover band playing his songs. Norah also performed—in disguises ranging from Batman to Eddie Munster to a bearded member of ZZ Top—with her indie rock band El Madmo. Daru Oda and Andy Borger, members of Norah's regular Handsome Band—rounded out El Madmo.

> **READ MORE**
> The Cannes Film Festival, which has been held annually for more than 60 years, is one of the world's largest and most important film festivals. For a brief description of the event, turn to page 49.

When not playing with her bands, Norah haunted New York's karaoke bars. Her karaoke specialties, she told an interviewer, are two very un-jazzy bands: the hard-rocking Guns N' Roses and Devo, an iconic punk group of the 1980s.

"My Dear Country"

In March 2008, Norah set aside kooky costumes and karaoke fun, turning her attention to serious political matters. Along with fellow musicians David Byrne, Moby, Lou Reed, Damien Rice, Laurie Anderson, and others, Norah played the Speak Up! Concert in Brooklyn, New York. The sold-out show was both a protest against the war in Iraq and a benefit for veterans of the war.

At the Speak Up! Concert, Norah performed "My Dear Country," which was particularly appropriate for the occasion. The song—written in the wake of the 2004 presidential voting—reveals Norah's dismay at the reelection of George W. Bush, who had made the costly decision to invade Iraq in 2003. But "My Dear Country" ends with an expression of patriotism and a tribute to freedom of speech:

> I love the things that you've given me,
> I cherish you my dear country,
> But sometimes I don't understand,
> The way we play.
>
> I love the things that you've given me,
> And most of all that I am free,
> To have a song that I can sing,
> On election day.

In the finest tradition of free speech in America, the artists who played the Speak Up! show were making it clear that they disagreed with President Bush and his policies.

Norah plays guitar at a benefit concert for the Bridge School, Mountain View, California, October 26, 2008. The Bridge School helps students with severe speech and physical impairments.

El Madmo

In May 2008, El Madmo's first album was released by Team Love, a small, independent record label based in New York. The self-titled album featured a dozen songs written by Norah and her band mates, Andy Borger and Daru Oda. They included "Vampire Guy," "Head in a Vise," "Attack of the Rock People," and "Nonny Goat Mon." Clearly, this was a departure from Norah's typical fare.

It was also a tongue-in-cheek effort, as El Madmo's MySpace page made clear—the band claimed to have been "born of social ineptitude and an ageless belief in trick-or-treatery." Still, some listeners complained that El Madmo didn't deliver genuine punk music. While most reviewers understood that the project was a lark, some didn't find it particularly funny. Others, however, were pleasantly surprised by the raw, raunchy, and wacky tunes, which played against Norah's customary low-key crooning.

Succeeding on Her Own Terms

With worldwide album sales of more than 35 million and counting, Norah Jones reigns as the 21st century's most commercially successful female recording artist. And she has built her career on her own terms. Unlike other top-selling female acts, Norah has refused to market her music by dressing or acting provocatively. She has avoided tabloid scandals. She appears uninterested in the trappings of fame or the high-profile life of a celebrity. For her, it seems, the music is the message.

Norah won millions of fans with a low-key, mellow kind of music. But she has boldly explored a variety of musical forms. Though she is still young, her music has already evolved significantly. Norah has shown that she is willing to take chances musically—and she isn't concerned about whether other people will approve. "It doesn't matter anymore if I'm completely understood," she told Jon Pareles of the *New York Times*. "Because you're not going to be. And you're never going to please everybody, so you shouldn't try."

Norah Jones sold more than 35 million albums worldwide before her 30th birthday, but she remains refreshingly modest and down-to-earth.

CROSS-CURRENTS

The Grammys

The Grammy Awards (named for the gramophone, an early device for playing sound recordings) honor artistic and technical achievements in the recording industry. They have been given annually since 1959 by the National Academy of Recording Arts & Sciences. Members of the Recording Academy, as it is popularly called, include singers, songwriters, producers, musicians, conductors, engineers, and other recording-industry professionals.

There are more than 100 Grammy categories. Each year, record companies and Recording Academy members submit thousands of entries for consideration. Experts screen each entry to ensure that it meets eligibility requirements and that it is put in the proper category. Then ballots are mailed to voting members of the Recording Academy. The first round of voting narrows the field down to five finalists in each category. A second round of voting determines the winners.

Whereas other music awards are based on fan voting or record sales, Grammy nominees are judged by their peers, and artistic and technical merit are supposed to be the only criteria. For this reason, winning a Grammy is considered a great honor among musical artists and producers.

Grammy winners are announced each year in February, during a star-studded, televised awards ceremony. The show includes live musical performances by nominees and other music luminaries.

The Grammy Award statuette, a symbol of musical excellence, is a golden gramophone. The gramophone was an early device for playing records.

CROSS-CURRENTS

The Queen of Soul

Aretha Franklin, nicknamed "the Queen of Soul," is a renowned performer. Born in Memphis, Tennessee, in 1942, she grew up in Detroit, Michigan. Her talent was evident from an early age. As a young girl, she sang in the church where her father was a pastor, wowing the congregation with powerful and passionate gospel solos.

By the age of 17, Franklin was an unwed mother with two sons. She decided to move to New York City to pursue a music career. It wasn't long before her talent attracted the attention of Columbia Records, which signed her to a recording contract in 1960.

Franklin's unique style fused soul, gospel, jazz, pop, and R&B. In a career that has spanned five decades, she has notched at least 45 *Billboard* Top 40 hits. Franklin has also garnered widespread critical acclaim. She has won more than 20 Grammy Awards. In 1987, she became the first woman inducted into the Rock and Roll Hall of Fame. In 2004, *Rolling Stone* magazine ranked her 1967 hit "Respect" number five on its list of the 500 greatest songs of all time. In 2008, when the magazine published its list of the 100 greatest singers of all time, Aretha Franklin was number one.

Aretha Franklin, circa 1970. *Rolling Stone* magazine ranked Franklin, who has more than 20 Grammy Awards to her credit, as the greatest singer of all time.

CROSS-CURRENTS

Ravi Shankar

Ravi Shankar, the father of Norah Jones, is India's most celebrated musician. He is a master of the sitar, a long-necked stringed instrument; a composer; and a leading scholar of classical Indian music.

Shankar was born in Varanasi, India, in 1920. In 1930, he went to Paris, where he attended school and performed with his older brother's dance troupe. After returning to India in the late 1930s, Shankar studied music under the famous teacher Allauddin Khan. By the late 1940s, Shankar had gained a reputation in India as a brilliant sitarist.

Shankar became an international celebrity after George Harrison of the British rock group the Beatles traveled to India in 1966 to study the sitar under him. The two became lifelong friends. In 1971, Shankar and Harrison organized the Concert for Bangladesh. Joined by other stars such as Bob Dylan, Eric Clapton, and Ringo Starr, they played two shows at New York City's Madison Square Garden to raise money for refugees in Bangladesh. Shankar also performed at two other iconic musical events from this era: the Monterey Pop Festival, held in 1967, and Woodstock, which took place in 1969.

Ravi Shankar has spent decades fusing Indian and Western musical traditions. His friend George Harrison called him "the Godfather of World Music."

Ravi Shankar in concert. The renowned sitar player is also an accomplished composer and a scholar of Indian classical music.

CROSS-CURRENTS

Billie Holiday

Jazz singer Billie Holiday was born Eleanora Fagan in Philadelphia on April 7, 1915. Soon after, her mother—an unmarried teen—moved to Baltimore, where Holiday spent most of her childhood. She grew up under difficult circumstances and dropped out of school in fifth grade.

In the late 1920s, Holiday went to New York, where she began singing in nightclubs. In 1933, she was discovered by the influential music producer John Hammond. Hammond introduced her to major jazz musicians, including Benny Goodman, with whom Holiday made her first commercial recording at the age of 18. A few years later, Holiday toured with the popular Count Basie Orchestra. A stint with the swing band of Artie Shaw was cut short because promoters balked at the idea of Holiday, an African American, touring with white musicians.

After that experience, Holiday pursued a solo career. With an intense, expressive vocal style, she won critical acclaim and commercial success. But her personal life was turbulent. A 1941 marriage ended in divorce, and she struggled with addiction. In 1947, she was sent to prison for drug possession. After her release the following year, Holiday resumed her recording career. She had some notable successes, but her heroin and alcohol addictions took a huge toll on her health. In 1959, Holiday died at the age of 44.

Jazz vocalist Billie Holiday enjoyed critical acclaim and commercial success, but she battled drug and alcohol addiction, dying at the age of 44.

CROSS-CURRENTS

Anoushka Shankar

Anoushka Shankar—the daughter of sitar virtuoso Ravi Shankar and his second wife, Sukanya Rajan—is a talented musician in her own right. Born in 1981, Anoushka spent much of her childhood in London, England, and in New Delhi, India, where the family had homes. Eventually, the Shankars settled in Encinitas, California.

When Anoushka was eight, Ravi Shankar presented his daughter with a custom-made, child-sized sitar. Under his tutelage, she learned to play the instrument and studied Indian classical music. By her teens, Anoushka was an accomplished musician. At the age of 13 she began appearing in concerts with her father, and she also made her recording debut on an album of his. She released the self-titled *Anoushka* (1998), her first solo album, a year before graduating from high school. It met with critical acclaim.

Typically in Indian culture, men play the sitar, while women accompany them through traditional song and dance. In 2000—the year Anoushka released her second album, *Anourag*—she blazed a new trail for Indian women by becoming the first female to play sitar at the famous Ramakrishna Center in Kolkata (formerly called Calcutta).

Anoushka's 2001 release, *Live at Carnegie Hall*, helped bring her music to an American audience. The

Anoushka Shankar before the 48th Grammy Awards, February 8, 2006. Her music blends Indian and Western styles.

record earned Anoushka a Grammy Award nomination for Best World Music Album. Her next album, *Rise* (2005), was also nominated for a Grammy. It highlighted Anoushka's diverse talents: in addition to performing, she produced the album and composed and arranged its songs. *Rise* also signaled a shift in Anoushka's music, from purely Indian styles to a more personal blend of Eastern and Western, classical and pop influences. Anoushka further explored that musical fusion with 2007's *Breathing Under Water*, a collaboration with Indian-American producer and musician Karsh Kale. Guest artists included Ravi Shankar, Sting, and—on the song "Easy"—Norah Jones.

Like her half sister, Anoushka has also tried her hand at acting. For her portrayal of a young dancer and bride in the 2004 movie *Dance Like a Man*, she was nominated for an Indian National Film Award. Anoushka has also written a biography of her famous father, *Bapi: The Love of My Life* (2002).

CROSS-CURRENTS

Dolly Parton

One of country music's best-loved performers, Dolly Parton has enjoyed a career spanning more than half a century. She was born on a farm in the mountains of Tennessee on January 19, 1946. One of 12 children of a poor sharecropper and his wife, Dolly grew up in a one-room cabin.

From her early childhood, she displayed musical ability, writing her first song at age five. By the time she was 10, Dolly had become a regular singer on local radio programs and on a television variety show broadcast from Knoxville, Tennessee.

Her first single was released in 1959. That same year, she made her debut at Nashville's Grand Ole Opry, the mecca of country music.

In 1967, Dolly Parton appeared on the *Billboard* country charts for the first time, recording her first #1 hit four years later. A string of #1 hits would follow, as Parton became one of country music's most popular performers. In 1978, she became the first female country singer to have a platinum album.

Country music legend Dolly Parton, 2007. Her career has spanned more than 50 years.

Parton has also made her mark as an actress. She has appeared in numerous television series and TV movies. Her big-screen credits include roles in the popular films *Nine to Five* (1980) and *Steel Magnolias* (1989).

Dolly Parton's many honors include multiple Grammys, two Academy Award nominations, and the Living Legend Medal from the Library of Congress.

CROSS-CURRENTS

The Cannes Film Festival

Cannes, a seaside city in southern France, has only about 80,000 permanent residents. But each year, for two weeks in May, the city's population doubles as thousands of actors, directors, producers, and journalists travel to the city for its famous film festival.

In 1939, the French minister for public instruction and the arts proposed the international film festival. But World War II broke out that year and lasted until 1945. As a result, the first Cannes Film Festival wasn't held until 1946.

In the beginning, the festival was simply a place where tourists came to see films. Prizes were given for nearly every movie shown. As the festival grew, however, the prizes became more important. Now there are only nine prizes awarded. The Palme d'Or Award, the most prestigious, is given for the best feature film. There are also prizes for direction, screenwriting, and acting.

Over the years, the Cannes Film Festival has become a significant place for movie studios to show their new films. Each year hundreds of films from all over the world are shown at the Cannes Film Festival, and winning at Cannes is a great honor.

Since 1946, the small city of Cannes, France, has been hosting a prestigious annual film festival.

Chronology

1979: Geetanjali Norah Jones Shankar is born in Brooklyn, New York.

1988: Moves to Grapevine, Texas, with her mother.

1995: Shortens her name to Norah Jones.

1996: Transfers from Grapevine High School to a Dallas-based magnet school, Booker T. Washington High School for the Performing and Visual Arts.

1997: Reconnects with her estranged father, international star Ravi Shankar, and meets her half sister, Anoushka Shankar, for the first time. Enrolls in the University of North Texas, where she majors in jazz piano.

1999: After her sophomore year of college, goes to New York City, intending to return to school in the fall. Instead, she decides to remain in New York, settling in the Greenwich Village neighborhood. Gradually meets the musicians who will form the Handsome Band. Meets Lee Alexander, who will be her boyfriend of over seven years.

2000: Auditions for Bruce Lundvall of Blue Note Records and lands a record deal.

2002: Debut album, *Come Away with Me*, is released.

2003: Wins five Grammy Awards; *Come Away with Me* wins three other Grammys.

2004: Second album, *Feels Like Home*, is released.

2007: Third album, *Not Too Late* is released. Stars in first film, *My Blueberry Nights*. Breaks up with Lee Alexander.

2008: In March, teams with other musicians to play the Speak Up! Concert, an antiwar benefit show. In May, Norah's indie band, El Madmo, releases its first self-titled album.

Awards and Achievements

Selected Discography
Come Away with Me (2002)
Feels Like Home (2004)
Not Too Late (2007)

With the Little Willies
The Little Willies (2006)

With El Madmo
El Madmo (2008)

Feature Film
My Blueberry Nights (2007)

Concert Films
Norah Jones: Live in New Orleans (2003)
Norah Jones and the Handsome Band—Live in 2004 (2004)

Awards
DownBeat Student Music Awards
> Best Original Composition (1996)
> Best Jazz Vocalist (1996, 1997)

Grammy Awards

Record of the Year (for "Don't Know Why"); 2003
Best Female Pop Vocal Performance (for "Don't Know Why"); 2003
Album of the Year (*Come Away with Me*); 2003
Best Pop Vocal Album (*Come Away with Me*); 2003
Best New Artist; 2003
Best Pop Collaboration with Vocals (with Ray Charles, for "Here We Go Again"); 2005
Record of the Year (for "Here We Go Again," with Ray Charles); 2005
Best Female Pop Vocal Performance (for "Sunrise"); 2005

Further Reading

Binelli, Marc. "The Accidental Superstar." *Rolling Stone*, February 25, 2004.

Colloff, Pamela. "No Fuss." *Texas Monthly*, vol. 32, issue 4 (April 2004).

Pareles, Jon. "Norah Jones: Now in Her Own Words." *New York Times*, January 21, 2007.

Ratliff, Ben. "Pop's Best Behaved." *New York Times*, February 8, 2004.

Internet Resources

http://www.norahjones.com/

Norah Jones's official Web site contains information about her band and discography, as well as touring news.

http://www.grammy.com/

The official Web site of the Grammy Awards has information about the awards, including current nominees and past winners.

http://www.pbs.org/jazz/time/time_women.htm

This page, part of the companion Web site for Ken Burns's documentary film *Jazz*, features profiles of great female jazz performers. It also includes audio samples.

http://www.cbsnews.com/stories/2007/02/08/60minutes/main2449673.shtml

Watch Katie Couric's *60 Minutes* interview with Norah Jones.

Publisher's Note: The Web sites listed on this page were active at the time of publication. The publisher is not responsible for Web sites that have changed their address or discontinued operation since the date of publication. The publisher reviews and updates the Web sites each time the book is reprinted.

Glossary

acclaim—praise; applause.

angst—a feeling of anxiety or dread.

collaboration—something (such as a musical or artistic project) done jointly with another person or with other people.

croon—to sing in a soft, smooth, often quiet style.

debut—a person's initial effort in a particular area (for example, the first music album).

demo—a sample recording in which an artist showcases his or her talents; short for "demonstration."

iconic—relating to someone or something that is widely admired as representative of a good type.

lyrics—the words of a song.

mesmerize—to hold spellbound; to capture the attention of a person as if by hypnosis.

prestigious—holding or reflecting considerable recognition, respect, or honor (as an award).

reconcile—to resolve differences and thereby restore a friendly relationship.

renowned—famous; celebrated.

sitar—a classical Indian stringed instrument that has a long neck.

Glossary

sophomore—a second-year student in high school or college; referring to the second year of high school or college; referring to an artist's second work.

statuette—a small statue, especially one given as an award or trophy.

sultry—passionate and alluring.

theatrics—flashy or showy gestures.

troupe—a group of theatrical performers.

venue—a place where performances (such as concerts) are held.

virtuoso—a highly skilled musician.

Chapter Notes

p. 9: "I can't believe this . . ." Leigh Johnson, "The 2003 Grammy Award Winners," *Hollywood.com*, February 24, 2003. http://www.hollywood.com/news/Norah_Jones_Is_Top_Grammy_Winner/1708317

p. 10: "I feel really blessed . . ." Billy Johnson Jr., "Norah Jones, Bruce Springsteen, Dixie Chicks Big Grammy Winners," *Yahoo! Music*, February 24, 2003. http://music.yahoo.com/read/news/12043618

p. 10: "I felt like I went . . ." Daniel Schorn, "The Humility of Norah Jones," *60 Minutes* online, February 11, 2007. http://www.cbsnews.com/stories/2007/02/08/60minutes/main2449673.shtml

p. 15: "It's probably one of . . ." Pamela Colloff, "No Fuss," *Texas Monthly*, vol. 32, issue 4 (April 2004): 60.

p. 16: "A soft-spoken girl . . ." Laura Smith, "Me and Norah Jones," *London Evening Standard*, May 9, 2003.

p. 17: "I used to be a jazz snob . . ." Jon Pareles, "Norah Jones, Now in Her Own Words," *New York Times*, January 21, 2007. http://www.nytimes.com/2007/01/21/arts/music/21pare.html?pagewanted=1

p. 17: "Usually people didn't listen . . ." Colloff, "No Fuss," 61.

p. 19: "I sang in some . . ." Pareles, "Norah Jones."

p. 20: "People are dipping . . ." Mark Binelli, "The Accidental Superstar," *Rolling Stone*, February 25, 2004. http://www.rollingstone.com/artists/norahjones/articles/story/5938337/the_accidental

Chapter Notes

p. 20: "She was playing . . ." Ibid.

p. 22: "First take, all live . . ." Lorraine Hahn, interview with Norah Jones, CNN.com *TalkAsia*, February 14, 2004. http://www.cnn.com/2004/WORLD/asiapcf/08/26/talkasia.jones.script/index.html

p. 23: "Norah Jones is truly . . ." Roger Crane, review of *Come Away with Me*, by Norah Jones. *All About Jazz*, June 11, 2002. http://www.allaboutjazz.com/php/article.php?id=1001

p. 25: "I was so overwhelmed . . ." Colloff, "No Fuss," 62.

p. 28: "kind of special . . ." Hahn, interview with Norah Jones.

p. 28: "Nothing much happens . . ." Ben Ratliff, "Pop's Best Behaved . . ." *New York Times*, February 8, 2004. http://query.nytimes.com/gst/fullpage.html?res=9C02EEDA153BF93BA35751C0A9629C8B63&sec=&spon=&pagewanted=all

p. 29: "I'm kind of nerdy . . ." Colloff, "No Fuss," 62.

p. 30: "darker, thornier, and sometimes . . ." Pareles, "Norah Jones."

p. 31: "You listen to my . . ." Michael Endelman, "Norah's Arc," *EW.com*, January 25, 2007. http://www.ew.com/ew/article/0,,20009699,00.html

p. 33: "I don't expect . . ." Schorn, "Humility of Norah Jones."

p. 34: "I thought, 'If I say . . ." Jake Coyle, "Norah Knows Why She Came to Film," *Yahoo! Music*, April 9, 2008. http://music.yahoo.com/ar-292258-news—Norah-Jones

p. 35: "It's like playing . . ." Reuters, "Norah Jones Brings Musical Touch to Movie Role," *Yahoo! Music*, April 2, 2008. http://music.yahoo.com/read/news/58953774

Chapter Notes

p. 36: "Ms. Jones, whose diffidence . . ." A. O. Scott, "On the Road, with Melancholia and a Hankering for Pie and Ice Cream," *New York Times*, April 4, 2008. http://movies.nytimes.com/2008/04/04/movies/04blue.html

p. 37: "may be a ripe . . ." Michael Phillips, review of *My Blueberry Nights*, directed by Wong Kar-wai, *Chicago Tribune*. http://www.baltimoresun.com/entertainment/movies/chi-18-my-blueberry-nights-review,0,6033280.story

p. 37: "We will always be . . ." "My Blueberry Nights—Norah Jones Interview," *IndieLondon Online*. http://www.indielondon.co.uk/Film-Review/my-blueberry-nights-norah-jones-interview

p. 40: "born of social ineptitude . . ." http://www.myspace.com/elmadmo

p. 42: It doesn't matter . . ." Pareles, "Norah Jones."

Index

Alexander, Lee, 20, 21, 28, 29, *30*, 37
"Attack of the Rock People," 40

Blue Note Records, 22, 26, 28, 30
Booker T. Washington High School, 15
Borger, Andy, 28, 29, 37, 40
Bridge School (California), *39*
Bush, George W., 32, 38

Campilongo, Jim, *30*
Cannes Film Festival, 35, *36*, 37, 49
Cash, Johnny, 14
Charles, Ray, 14
Come Away with Me, 9–10, 22–23, 28, 29, 33
Couric, Katie, 32–33
"Creepin' In," 27

"Don't Know Why," 7, 8, 9–10, 21, 22–23, 24–25
"Don't Miss You at All," 27
DownBeat Student Music

Awards, 15–16

Ellington, Duke, 23, 27
El Madmo, 37, 40

Feels Like Home, 26–28, 29, 33
Franklin, Aretha, 8, 9, 20, 43

Grammy Awards, 6–11, 42
Grapevine (TX) High School, 15

Handsome Band, 20–21, 22, 23–24, 26, 27–28
Harris, Jesse, 10, 21
Harrison, George, *13*, 44
"Head in a Vise," 40
Holiday, Billie, 14, 23, 45
Hoskulds, S. Husky, 10

Interlochen Arts Camp, 14, 21

Jones, Norah
 acting career, 34–37
 benefit concerts played by, 38, *39*

Numbers in ***bold italics*** refer to captions.

Index

birth, 12
childhood, 12–16
and critical response to her music, 23, 26–27, 28, 30–31, 40
and *DownBeat* Student Music Awards, 15–16
early professional career, 16, 17, 18–22
education, 14–16, 17, 18, 21
and El Madmo, 37, 40
fame, attitude toward, 24–25, 28–29
Grammy Awards won by, 8, **9**, 10, **11**
and jazz, 15, 17, 23
and karaoke, 37, 38
and Little Willies, 29, 30, 37
musical influences of, 14–16, 17, 27, 31–32
parents, 12, 13–14, 16, 24, 44
personal philosophy, 25, 30–31, 40–41
record sales, 23, 26, 33, 40
romantic interests, 20, 29, 37
tours, 23–24, 28
Jones, Sue (mother), 12, 13–14
Julian, Richard, **30**

Kar-wai, Wong. *See* Wong Kar-wai

Law, Jude, 35, **36**
Levy, Adam, 20, 28
Little Willies, 29, **30**, 37
Living Room, 21–22
Lundvall, Bruce, 22

Mardin, Arif, 8, **9**, 10, 29
Mitchell, Joni, 14
My Blueberry Nights, 34–37
"My Dear Country," 38

Nelson, Willie, 14, 29, 30, 37
Newland, Jay, 8, 10
"Nonny Goat Mon," 40
Not Too Late, 30, 31–32, 33

Oda, Daru, 14, 21, 28, 29, 37, 40

Parton, Dolly, 14, 27, 48
Portman, Natalie, 35

Raitt, Bonnie, 8, 9
Rieser, Dan, **30**

Shankar, Anoushka (sister), 16–17, 46–47
Shankar, Ravi (father), 12, **13**, 16, 24, 44, 46
"Sinkin' Soon," 32
Speak Up! Concert, 38
Strathairn, David, 35

Team Love, 40

University of North Texas

Index

(UNT), 17, 21

"Vampire Guy," 40
Van Zandt, Townes, 27

Waits, Tom, 27

Weisz, Rachel, 35
"Wish I Could," 32
Wonder, Stevie, 14
Wong Kar-wai, 34

Photo Credits

- 7: Kevin Mazur/WireImage/Getty Images
- 9: Frank Micelotta/Getty Images
- 11: Steve Granitz/WireImage/Getty Images
- 13: Michael Ochs Archives/Stringer/Getty Images
- 15: Seth Poppel Yearbook Library
- 16: Theo Wargo/WireImage/Getty Images
- 19: AP Photo/Jim Cooper
- 21: AP Photo/Scout Tufankjian
- 24: AP Photo/Darko Bandic
- 27: Scott Gries/Getty Images
- 30: AP Photo/Jim Cooper
- 31: Michael Crabtree/Bloomberg News/Landov
- 35: © The Weinstein Company/Photofest
- 36: AP Photo/Kirsty Wigglesworth
- 39: Steve Jennings/WireImage/Getty Images
- 41: AP Photo/Evan Agostini
- 42: Steve Granitz/WireImage for NARAS/Getty Images
- 43: Michael Ochs Archives/Stringer/Getty Images
- 44: Raveendran/Stringer/AFP/Getty Images
- 45: Michael Ochs Archives/Getty Images
- 46: Timothy A. Clary/AFP/Getty Images
- 48: Used under license from Shutterstock, Inc.
- 49: Used under license from Shutterstock, Inc.

Cover Images:
Main Image: Jim Spellman/WireImage/Getty Images
Top Inset: Ron Wolfson/WireImage/Getty Images
Bottom Inset: Ryan Born/WireImage/Getty Images

About the Author

DONNA LATHAM is an award-winning author and playwright who received the ASPCA Henry Bergh Children's Book Award for her nonfiction work *Fire Dogs*. Her favorite Norah Jones songs are "Sinkin' Soon" and "My Dear Country." Like Norah Jones, Donna has been greatly influenced by a rip-roaring gaggle of bold women.